MEHRAB AND GRACIE

MEHRAB AND GRACIE

Jane Graham

ARTHUR H. STOCKWELL LTD
Torrs Park, Ilfracombe, Devon, EX34 8BA
Established 1898
www.ahstockwell.co.uk

© *Jane Graham, 2020*
First published in Great Britain, 2020

The moral rights of the author have been asserted.

*All rights reserved.
No part of this publication may be reproduced
or transmitted in any form or by any means,
electronic or mechanical, including photocopy,
recording, or any information storage and
retrieval system, without permission
in writing from the copyright holder.*

*British Library Cataloguing-in-Publication Data.
A catalogue record for this book is available
from the British Library.*

*This is a work of fiction. Names, characters, places and incidents are
the product of the author's imagination and any resemblance to actual
persons, living or dead, events or locales, is purely coincidental.*

ISBN 978-0-7223-5041-6
*Printed in Great Britain by
Arthur H. Stockwell Ltd
Torrs Park   Ilfracombe
Devon EX34 8BA*

MEHRAB AND GRACIE

PART ONE

"My name is Mehrab. I'm here to meet you and take you to your hotel."

I was relieved to be met, and by this pleasant-looking man with a gravelly voice.

He took my suitcase and said, "What have you come here for, Ida Grace? You are the first visitor to set foot in this place for six months. The war has completely spoiled tourism."

"It's cold standing out here in the wind. Let's get into your car and chat there," I said, though I couldn't see a car anywhere.

"OK, but do you mind coming on my motorbike? There is a curfew in the town prohibiting cars and buses from midday to midnight."

I laughed. "I don't mind at all – in fact, it might be fun. But what shall I do with my suitcase?"

I noticed a different, happy side to him now, a twinkle in his eye. He was obviously relieved when he realised that I wasn't going to complain about riding pillion on the bike, and that I might even enjoy it. We walked over to the bike, an ancient but well-kept

Harley-Davidson, and he called to a man wrapped in a blanket under a nearby tree.

"Take this to the hotel, Hamid," he said, pointing to my bright-red-and-yellow striped suitcase.

He and Hamid then had a lengthy exchange with much frowning that ended with Mehrab pointing to a small string of coloured glass beads I was wearing around my neck.

"Do you mind giving Hamid your bead necklace?" he asked. "No good paying Hamid money to carry your bag. These days money will be stolen from him before he reaches the hotel. He says he'd rather have your beads."

I was surprised and a bit puzzled by the request. I was fond of the beads. They were given to me by an old woman when I was working in the Namib Desert. I had carried her back to her hut because she'd twisted her ankle rounding up her goats. I didn't really want to part with the beads. However, not wanting to cause any ill feeling I said, "OK, why not? I should be delighted." And I undid the clasp. "There we go," I said as the beads fell into my hand.

I gave them to Hamid who giggled, very happy, and immediately put them on.

"I believe these to be lucky beads Hamid, so look after them." I joked.

"Oh, Hamid, that looks good," said Mehrab. "Maybe I will swap them with you for a hot meal when we get to the hotel."

Hamid was a very thin man and could obviously do with a good, hot meal.

He put the suitcase on his head and said to Mehrab,

"Well, that's up to you, sir," and off he went just as a light snow began to fall.

It was supposed to be the beginning of spring, so the weather should be warming up soon.

'I'm looking forward to that,' I thought to myself. 'It'll be cold on the bike ride.'

I was glad I was wearing my leather skirt and jacket for warmth and I noticed that Mehrab was wearing old, well-worn leathers to keep himself warm.

"Hop on," Mehrab urged, handing me a helmet and pointing impatiently to the bike.

He was obviously feeling the cold too. I felt a little tinge of anxiety and decided to make sure this man whom I'd only just met really was going to take me to my hotel.

"Before we take off on your bike in the snowstorm, who are you, Mehrab, and what do you do here?"

He laughed and said, "Don't worry, Ida Grace – I'm a businessman, but I'm also the caretaker of the hotel. That's how I know your name." He paused, and smiled at me. "OK, now it's your turn to tell me what you are up to. How do I know you aren't going to shoot me in the back on the way to the hotel on my bike. What are you really doing here, Ida Grace? International tourism is just a joke these days."

"I'm here to write a book. I need somewhere where I can be alone when I need to. No tourists, no visitors suits me fine."

As we got going he turned and shouted happily, "I shall be the hero of your story."

It took about thirty minutes to get to the hotel. The

streets were deserted save for a scattering of cold soldiers, who were alerted by the grumble of the Harley as we passed by. The mountains surrounding the town were blanketed in snow. It was so quiet and peaceful – no sign of war at all.

A few kilometres from the airport we turned on to a narrow, windy road, very slippery, so difficult to negotiate. We crawled along at a snail's pace, but finally crept up a small hill and arrived at the main entrance of the Sheer Magic Hotel. It was magic too. I stared breathlessly at the mountain views. The hotel was surrounded by snow-capped peaks. From the hotel's main entrance, terraced gardens had been cultivated as far as the eye could see. The hotel itself looked empty of tourists.

"Is it possible that I am the only guest in this magnificent palace?" I spoke out loud.

One of a small group of friendly-looking staff answered my question: "No tourists at the moment, but there are always a few local people and business travellers."

Then they all approached me and shook my hand as I went in to the lobby. Hamid was one of them. I wondered how he'd managed to get there before us.

Hamid took me through the lobby into a tea lounge, where he suggested I should have a cup of tea to warm myself up. But I wanted to keep going – it was all so exciting – and so I followed Hamid up the stairs to the first floor, Room 111. That wouldn't be difficult to remember.

It was a splendid room, light and airy. It must have been around sixty square metres, plus a wide balcony that overlooked the gardens and mountains. The décor was simple and artistic with numerous traditional storyboards adorning the walls. All the little tables sported assorted handicrafts – woven cloths, bamboo lamps and coconut-shell bowls. The adjoining bathroom was about as big as the small mud house I'd been living in just before coming here. I'd spent two years in that little room and it had been a friendly home, from where I'd caught scorpions for some kinky biologist working in the Namib Desert. Now I was lost in luxury, but a knock on the door brought me back to reality. It was Mehrab.

"I hope you will be happy here, Ida Grace. Let me know if there is anything you need." He paused and said, "If you don't mind me saying, you do have a very strange name." He winked at me.

"No, I don't mind what you say. I'm impervious to that sort of thing. I could say the same about you. I won't though because I know where the name Mehrab comes from. It's the name of the King of Kabul in the Shahname – a Persian name in the Book of Kings. How is that for knowledge?" I stared at him and raised my right eyebrow.

He winked again.

"I hope you don't object to me winking at you. It's an uncontrollable habit of mine – nothing sinister."

"I have never objected to a wink or two. It can be very endearing," I laughed.

"You are a very smart lady. We must sit on your verandah sometime and play questions and answers. Round here we play to the same rules as strip poker."

He was gone before I could react.

As he left the room I wondered about him. Yes, caretaker was believable, but I wondered what he'd meant by 'businessman' – the traditional answer that covered everything and explained nothing. He was tall, well built and good-looking with heavy dark eyebrows and brown eyes. He had a Roman nose that in the early days in Persia signified beauty and nobility. His short black hair was slicked back with oil and his small sideburns turned into fashionable stubble. He had full lips that gave him a permanent pouting expression. He could be anyone from a fashion designer to the owner of all the hotels for miles around, a big-time crook, a secret agent, a black-market trader, or just a nice guy wasting his life in a dozy backwater. What sort of trader could he be and how on earth could there be any trade here in this area where everything seemed to be shut down? He would have to be in the black market. Whatever! I couldn't help feeling there was something mysterious about him. Well, I didn't mind – he seemed pleasant company and I had to admit I found him rather attractive. Little did I realise at the time that he was always on the move, no doubt getting himself involved in all manner of very risqué ventures. And obviously he was a dab hand at getting out of them too. He was a free man when it came to making money. He had no family, so he had nothing to lose.

A new life began for me that day – the day of my arrival at the aptly named Sheer Magic Hotel. It was very different to my life hitherto, working in African national parks, helping with research and taking tourists on safari. That had been an interesting life, but it had come to a sudden end. Now, in this amazing place, I could do what I'd always dreamed of doing full-time: art and writing. It was a bonus to be surrounded by friendly people and sometimes to see Mehrab. The staff were terrified that one day the hotel would be bombed, even though I'd been told before I came that the war scarcely affected this part of the country. I told them it would never happen, even though I had no real idea and they were happy to hear that from me; it gave them confidence.

Little did I realise at the time that Mehrab was often away. The military obviously gave him free passage to come and go as he pleased. On his return to the hotel I never asked him where he'd been. I was always happy to see him come back in one piece. We spent happy, good fun times together, wandering around the garden, arguing about the names of the flowers. The immediate area was dotted with small lakes and beautiful forest. We loved to potter around in a canoe or in the forest. We became good friends, never at a loss for words; there were rarely any long embarrassing silences, always so much to talk about. He showed me all his favourite places in the town, and around.

Gradually we became enamoured of each other, and the days we weren't together grew to be lonely days. Nevertheless, I tried to enjoy every day, and was inspired by my surroundings. I kept busy. Unusually, new ideas seemed to tumble from me like coins from a casino fruit machine.

Mehrab was well respected by the staff at the hotel and by the occasional visitors. He left Hamid in charge in his absence. He had learnt all the tricks of the trade from Mehrab so there were never any serious problems.

Hamid introduced me to the work at the hotel reception desk and to some of his friends at a nearby orphanage that I visited frequently to play with the children. I enjoyed these new activities and even found it relaxing and fun to change my routines and meet more people. I started to build things from found objects as my art materials were running out fast and there was no way I could buy replacements in the lifeless town. Hamid and some of the other staff became interested in creating objects too, and we often came to work with bags full of bits of wood and metal, broken coloured glass, feathers and broken table cutlery. We put all the equipment from one of the games rooms into the next-door room and created a workshop for ourselves. The experimental, random work gave me something more to think about in life, as well as more artistic freedom than my conventional oil painting and book writing. Teaching Hamid and the boys some of the tricks of the trade was fun too. Now and then a visitor to the hotel would buy one of the creations and that really encouraged the would-be artists.

On Mehrab's return from a long trip he always came straight to my room. He thought of me as his wild girl because of the life I had previously led in the bush in Africa.

His first words to me as he entered my room were always the same: "Stay wild and untamed. You should be my full-time partner in crime – I get lonely without you."

I would throw my head back and laugh and remind him of his own secretive ways and joke that I had no idea what crime he was talking about so how could I be a partner? He would pull me close to him and tell me I was his champion. But he never asked me to join him on a trip. And it never occurred to me that I should leave the hotel and move on to another place. It was always irrelevant once he got back. We just fell back into our wonderful routine, spending long hours of the day together, chatting, laughing, walking, playing music and getting to know more about each other. I even stopped worrying about whether he was a full-time crook or not, going off, disguising himself and buying and selling drugs or something else. I thought it was just my imagination. I never failed to tell him how lonely I was without him.

"I get lonely. I don't like not knowing where you are. Life isn't the same without you."

He'd put his arms around me saying, "I'm always beside you, honey."

It pacified me to hear him call me honey. It made me feel that he really cared about me, but it gradually became more difficult for both of us. Frequently I would cry when he left to go somewhere – something I had never done since I was a little girl – and he reassured me that he would not be doing many more long trips.

I had been in the Sheer Magic Hotel for a year when Mehrab asked me if I thought it would be fun to take a trip somewhere together. He suggested a visit to one of the larger lakes in an area sixty kilometres from the hotel. He had already checked everything out with the military and we were free to go whenever we wanted to. It was the end of spring and all the mountain snow was melting, so, according to Mehrab, that meant the lake would be at its best, having filled up from the melt.

We packed his old Land Rover and headed to the lake. The lake – Lake Plato – had been a favourite for tourists before the military action in the area. Apparently there had been twelve small sailing boats there and we hoped we would find them in good condition so we could sail up the lake. I was very excited. I had spent a lot of time on one sort of boat or another in the past, canoeing in the Bangweulu Swamp in Zambia to photograph black lechwe; canoeing at night in the Okavango Delta in Botswana, catching crocodiles; travelling in the rescue boat for one of the crews in the annual canoe race from Molokai to Kauai in Hawaii; and canoeing with a group of people up the Zambezi River in Zimbabwe to the Mozambique border. Every boat trip was exciting, even the long-haul journeys when I was a child going to England from Kenya around the Cape of Good Hope.

Mehrab and I arrived at Lake Plato in the late afternoon. It was encouraging to find that some yachts were still functional, tied up at an old wooden jetty. A wizened old man who called himself Mishak came to meet us. He seemed as excited to see us as we were to see him. He had made his home on one of the boats, but there were still several to choose from. We presumed he was a government game scout. He said he hadn't seen any tourists for months and told us to choose one of the boats straight away so that he could get it ready before dark. The boats were almost identical and I made a choice straight away. The boat was called *Kintekinte*. I told Mehrab that the name of the boat meant 'fast' in Portuguese Creole spoken in Guinea-Bissau, where I had made some short trips travelling in a small jet boat of the same name in the Bijagós Archipelago. Mehrab was surprised to hear me speak of Guinea-Bissau. He told me he used to have a friend there who had been shot in a political skirmish with a neighbouring country a few years back. He had visited his friend there and they had hired a small fishing canoe for an afternoon's fishing and that was called *Kintekinte*. It sank so they had to swim to shore.

"We didn't go anywhere fast in that canoe," he laughed.

Mishak then told us that a Portuguese tourist had given the name to our boat because he, sailing in that boat, always won the boat races that he and his group used to have on the lake during their holiday there. Mehrab made a joke that I shouldn't have chosen a boat with the name of *Tinky Tinky* because the name implied that it might have some loose nuts and bolts.

"Well, I'm not worried about that – you are here to fix it if necessary. I know you are an experienced sailor."

"How do you know?" asked Mehrab.

"Well, you look like a sailor with all that long hair and whiskers around your face. Why do you change your look every now and then, from the city look, clean-shaven, as in many of your photographs, to the rough-as-a-bear look, when you are almost unrecognisable. How do I know it's you?"

"Well, it's a seasonal change in looks, for winter. The winter look. Now that it's spring and the temperature is going up, this look will be too hot, so I shall be shaving off the long hair and whiskers soon. Besides, I don't want you to get bored with me, so I am banking on a new look to keep you interested."

"How do I know it's the same you?"

"You will know when I kiss you."

We laughed. Then there was a long silence as I pondered again over who was he really and what did he do? Was he trying to disguise himself?

He broke the silence and came up to me and put his arm around me, saying, "I want to make another change too. Can I call you Gracie? Ida Grace is such a mouthful. I want to get rid of all the wrapping and see you laid bare for me, in more ways than one!"

I looked serious. I loved him, but as a friend. When he went away I was always so depressed, but when he was with me I didn't want to think anything more of him than as my best friend. I wanted to be with him but, at the same time, to be free to come and go if I wanted. The reason I only wanted to stay as a friend at this stage and not get too involved was that three years ago I had had a stillborn child in a previous relationship. I still hadn't got over this tragic event. I felt it was a natural reaction to want to spend some time to sort myself out and heal my mind and body before getting involved in a new serious relationship. I had to tell Mehrab about this when a suitable opportunity arose. This wasn't the right moment, but it jarred my memory when he spoke of seeing me laid bare. I didn't say anything and Mehrab stared me straight in the eye.

"You and I will always have unfinished business. Whether we are together or apart I feel I have a heart-related connection with you. When I hear from you when I am travelling it makes me smile and I feel genuine happiness and positive feelings. I hope you always stay safe and don't go off on any of your adventures and leave me when I am away. I will miss you. So, let's get back to the original question: please can I call you Gracie?"

What he said brought tears to my eyes.

"Of course you can call me Gracie," I spluttered, stretching my arm around him and giving him a big kiss on the cheek.

We went and sat on the jetty with a cool bag full of buttered bread and salad. It wasn't long before we were interrupted by Mishak, the boatman.

"The boat is ready, Mehrab. Come and look."

We wandered off to check out the boat and make arrangements for the early morning start.

I wasn't very tired when we finally crawled into our sleeping bags. A short time later I heard Mehrab snoring. In the lamplight I noticed how cosy the cabin looked with bunk beds covered with bright African materials. There was lots of space, unlike some sailing boats that were so rammed tight with cupboards, radio and map desks and cooking gear it was hard to breathe. Of course there was no emergency radio in the craft, but it would be easy to swim to the shore if necessary. There was a neat little toilet, but as far as I was concerned pumping a cabin loo was out of the question. Pumping these loos is comparable to thirty minutes in the gym, and that is once you have remembered which taps to turn on or off and in what order. A better option would be to make use of a patch of reeds on a sandbank. The breeze in the shrouds of the boats created a mournful, strange noise like a flock of some exotic wild seabirds or birds of paradise on a faraway river. I felt excited by it all.

Then Mehrab spoke: "Gracie, are you sleeping?"

"No."

"Come and lie with me and keep me warm?"

"OK, why not? I'll bring my sleeping bag or we won't have room to . . . breathe."

It was the right thing to do and we were asleep in no time.

We started on the journey up the lake at dawn, having said goodbye to Mishak.

"We are quite a sight," said Mehrab, his mouth full of ham and cheese. "You see, Gracie, neither of us is wearing the correct sailing gear." He laughed. "Your leopard-spotted hat isn't very nautical. And those granny glasses make you look quite out of the ordinary."

"What do you mean by that?"

"You look goofy. Not the usual suave, energetic, intelligent, sexy blonde, wearing a leather jacket and short leather skirt above the knees, beating up the town on a Harley-Davidson."

"You haven't seen anything yet!"

When we got going into the wind I was impressed to see how everything in the cabin was on swivels so that it all hung horizontal even when the boat heeled over. I wished that I could be suspended in the same sort of mechanism because I was feeling a bit dizzy with love. I noticed as we sailed along how beautiful the lake was, and the scene was spectacular. Huge water lilies grew as far as the eye could see and the water itself seemed to change colour in the different light throughout the day. I acknowledged it by nodding and breathing deeply.

"Gracie, are you happy?"

"Yes, I am as happy as I can be, although I'm not a lover of lush green riverbanks or green forests like you are. I love the desert, the dead sticks, the sand dunes," I said. "This is a great second best," I teased.

We stopped a few times and pulled the boat up on to the shore, scattering a number of otters playing vigorously in the water on one occasion. They were rolling and frolicking around. Mehrab suggested we might do the same and take the opportunity to have a wash and a swim.

"Doesn't the water here look a bit murky for a swim?"

We dived in anyway.

"I normally only wash in rose water."

"I know – I've noticed the sweet smell in your room at the hotel. And besides that, you always smell sweet and you are a sweet lady!"

I laughed. "I am a natural woman – no hairs, but sleek like the otters and no gracies, as my name is Ida Grace!" So that's why I am a natural woman: no airs, no gracies.

"Ha ha Gracie – no airs and no graces." He giggled. "You are not a natural woman either – you are supernatural!"

I found a lump of mud on the bank and threw it at him. A battle ensued, chasing after each other like the otters, swimming, diving and corkscrewing around.

"My taste is like the otters," he laughed. "All this twisting and lunging! I love long-timing (a Mehrab word) pleasures and I hate to do things in a hurry. After all their vigorous play otters normally copulate for up to thirty minutes, so I am told. What do you think about that, Gracie?"

"No deal," I replied.

Then I told him about my previous relationship, the stillborn child, the emotional agony and physical pain, and how I was trying to get back to normal. I wasn't frigid and I was in no way disinterested – far from it. I was just waiting for the perfect moment.

"I hope you will be patient, honey."

"My dear, Gracie, you should have told me before. There is no rush. Of course I will wait patiently. As it is, our journey here on the lake is laced with embraces, kisses and more. Our own journey is one that I don't want to come to an end; I like you a lot, Gracie. You are so wise and kind and clever. I love your sense of humour and you are so loving. I will wait for the perfect moment too. I can wait until the cows come home, which could be a very long time as we don't even own any cows at the moment."

I felt as though we had made a deal. It seemed that I loved him and he loved me. All I wanted was to seal the deal then and there, but I was still not certain. He picked me up, cradled me in his arms and kissed me.

On the third day around midday we dropped the anchor and tied the boat up at a small jetty.

"Let's prolong this fairy-tale trip," Mehrab said. "If we sit here a while I am pretty sure that a game scout will turn up. You see, Gracie, this end of the lake borders on a small national park. It is an amazing place. Let's wait around. I know there are a few cabins about a mile from here. If someone turns up we can get them to look after the boat and we will walk to the cabins and spend a few nights here."

"Wow, that sounds like a plan."

I was thrilled. It was very smoky in the area and I wondered if there was a bush fire burning. Mehrab wasn't bothered by it, saying that we could find out about that if someone turned up.

"If they don't come, we'll spend the night here and make our way back tomorrow. I hear burning trees, but see red roses for me and you. What do you think?"

He winked. I loved his wink, which he often seemed to do when he was willing something to happen, like having the man turn up so we could spend some more time together.

Assigid turned up mid-afternoon with a younger man tagging along.

"Welcome to Village Park," he said, and before we could answer he started on a long description of the place, just as he was accustomed to do with tourists. "Village Park got its name because there used to be three big villages here that were moved to another area to make a park here . . . grasslands . . . rocky outcrops

". . . cliffs . . . coniferous pine forest . . . waterfalls . . . coloured flowers . . ."

Each feature was spoken mechanically, one after the other, as though he was saying it all as he was marching along. Mehrab and I were impressed by the presentation, but bored by the length of the spiel.

Finally Assigid stopped and said, "Any questions, sir?"

Mehrab replied, "No, no, all very interesting and –"

Much to Mehrab's dismay Assigid kept going: ". . . animal species . . . deer . . . leopard . . . black and brown bears . . . twenty-three bird species. Any questions, sir?"

Here Mehrab took his chance and asked Assigid if the ecotourist cabins were operating. Was it possible to walk to them or was there a fire burning in the park? If we walked in, could the other young man look after the boat for a few days?

"Yes, sir, the cabins are functioning with one staff member who will cook, clean and tidy. There is basic food in the camp kitchen so there is no need to carry your food in. There has been a big fire burning in the park some distance away but it is only smouldering now so we can walk to the cabins."

Then he stopped and he and the other young man conversed for a good ten minutes.

Finally he said, "Fodro will look after the boat for you for a few days. He says he would like that bead necklace you are wearing, sir, in exchange."

I'd noticed when we set out on the trip that Mehrab was wearing the beads I had given to Hamid. Mehrab had obviously swapped them for 'a good hot meal' at the hotel on the day I'd arrived. Now Fodro wanted it and Mehrab didn't want to give it to him. He told Fodro that he was very sorry but he could not give him the beads. I was surprised, but at the same time I was pleased that Mehrab wanted to keep them. I chuckled under my breath. Fodro looked glum and for a few minutes there was a stony silence. Then he spoke to Assigid, who passed the message on.

"He says alternatively he will take your watch and a handful of madam's shiny hair."

Surprised, I thought that was more peculiar than Hamid asking for the beads in the very beginning. Hair was easy, but not a handful. I would have to control the haircut. I took a small pair of scissors out of my daypack, cut a lock of hair and put it into Fodro's hand. He was shaking with excitement. Then I gave him a cloth bag to put it in, but he threw that in the lake and put the hair under the cap he was wearing. Mehrab had already given him his favourite very old watch. We both felt the deal was well worth it, giving us the chance to spend time in the park. The deal was done.

Fodro climbed on to the boat and Mehrab and I followed Assigid to the cabins. It was a cold spring evening and the walk took us almost an hour. It was an invigorating walk, running some of the time, chasing and trying to catch butterflies and then trying to catch each other, like kids let loose to look for Easter eggs in a hardware store. We were pleased to be off the boat for a while and making the most of the open space, leaping over rocks, falling down and clutching at each other tightly as we got ourselves upright again.

Assigid failed to see the point in any of it and kept pestering us to get into line. Eventually we came to heel and trudged along behind him.

On arrival at the cabins another old park retainer met us. Assigid introduced him as Thomas, who cooked, cleaned and tidied. He spoke a few words to Thomas, who nodded and then shook hands with us. Mehrab was sure they were discussing the sleeping arrangements. He was correct because he showed Mehrab to the furthest-away cabin and I had the cabin near the living area. The old men were obviously discussing the fact that we were not married.

Toasted cheese and rice was a welcome evening meal and we washed it down with a few glugs of dark rum, which Mehrab had brought from the boat. It was the fashionable drink with the young men in the Sheer Magic Hotel. Mehrab didn't want Fodro to get his hands on that.

I felt lonely in my cabin that night, having got used to sharing the boat cabin with Mehrab. I heard a leopard calling in the distance. It reminded me of Africa in the past – the undisciplined life I'd led before, and how it had all ended when I inadvertently fell pregnant. When the baby was stillborn I tried to settle down, take a different path, so I found more conventional employment, working in a laboratory as a wildlife researcher, rather than working for a big travel company out in the bush. Also, I began writing about my experiences as well as describing them in paint. However, I had spent the last two years collecting scorpions in the Namib Desert, which was not very conventional. It had been a quiet life and I'd enjoyed making friends with the Namib Desert women. I told them about life in my world and they taught me about the desert. I wouldn't get that opportunity again.

The last few months in the desert were very difficult for me. One day a man from the nearest town brought me an express letter from South Africa. It had been written four months before, but had taken all that time to reach me. The letter was from my parents' neighbours, who were also their best friends. The letter begged me to come home immediately. They described a robbery at my parents' home. All the family had been asleep at night when a gang of thieves broke into the house. The atrocities of the robbery as they described them to me were so horrific that I couldn't even finish reading the letter. My father and mother and the twins were hacked to death. Everyone was dead. I was so shocked I couldn't imagine what to do next. I howled and shut myself away in the little hut for a day. Sitting there alone, I suddenly realised that there was nothing I could do; it was four months later. Even the funeral was over. I had no desire to go home and relive the horrors of what the neighbours had recounted. I was better off finishing what I was doing and then decide when to go back. I wanted to keep the happy memories of my family with me as I always did. I wanted to ignore the terrible news and live my life as though nothing had happened. I didn't even answer the letter.

When the scorpion job was over, I still had no idea of what path to take. I decided to resolve it by leaving my decision to chance. I didn't want to take any responsibility for my life. A stillborn child, my family murdered – how could I make a responsible decision about my future life? I stood in my desert hut, took out a map of the world and spread it on my bed. I soaked my thumb with ink from the ink pad. I shut my eyes. I would carefully turn around twice, bend over and make a mark with my thumb on the map. I would go there next.

Whilst turning around I tripped over a shoe lying by the bed and fell on to the bed, crumpling the map. Nevertheless, I followed through with my plan and firmly pressed my thumb down somewhere on the map. I found I was on my way to Pakistan, to an area that had been at war with neighbouring countries for some years. That didn't put me off. I had lived under these circumstances before in Ethiopia.

I left my desert hut. I studied some maps and found a place where I believed there would be solitude – a quiet life with no commitments, where I could write and paint and get to grips with myself again. I was headed for the Sheer Magic Hotel. I met Mehrab.

Now after a year we were close friends, enjoying a few days together in Village National Park. Tripping over the shoe in the Namib Desert hut was the best thing that could have happened to me.

On the spur of the moment, I decided to go to him in spite of what our hosts might think. I knew which cabin he was in. I found him sleeping. I slipped off my sarong and crept under the blanket with him. He was nude. He was so warm. I pulled him towards me and held his body very close and kissed him and we locked ourselves in a firm embrace.

Mehrab whispered in my ear: "I would love to cover you with my body."

I laughed to myself at his funny English.

Not knowing why I was laughing he said, "It's important to me, Gracie." He squeezed me tight.

"You are too sexy for me," I teased. "Besides, covering my body could mean something different to each of us. I am guessing though that you and I do often interpret words in the same way. Just a guess. But not this time."

"Your guess is always right, babe," he replied.

He didn't mention it again, but we slept in the same cabin every night after that much to Assigid's and Thomas's quiet disapproval.

Each day in the park we made a plan with Assigid about what to do and where to go. We decided to choose a particular area daily hoping to find certain animals there.

The first day we started off in the direction of a line of small kopjes, in search of leopards. Assigid said that although they were quite common, they were very secretive, hiding in the rocks.

"They see us, but we not see them."

To get to the kopjes we had to cross an area of long, dry grass.

After ten minutes I said to Mehrab, "Wow, I thought I was fit. I'm already exhausted."

He suggested that as he was taller than I was it was much easier for him; and besides, I probably wasn't fit because I didn't involve myself in enough night-time activities. I would have none of his teasing, but agreed that he would find it easier because he was tall. The long grass was halfway up my legs, so I couldn't walk through it, but had to step over it. Jokingly I pleaded with Assigid to carry me.

"If we find an elephant, I will ask him to carry you, Gracie."

In spite of Assigid's severe disciplinary ways he was friendly and had a guarded sense of humour. He was bush-savvy too and we enjoyed his company.

Just before we reached the kopje, Assigid, who was in front, stopped abruptly and pointed. "Shh-h! Look, leopard, climb hill, going slow, maybe with cub."

'He has the eyes of a sniper,' Mehrab thought as neither he nor I could see the animal.

Then Assigid said that it had disappeared. "It sit down now under tree. It come from hunting maybe. We sit down now under tree and wait."

We waited for half an hour, then Assigid suggested we come back early the next day.

"Get here, this place and watch."

We did that for the two following mornings, but we had no luck. On our last morning in the park we headed towards a larger kopje further away, but it was easier to reach. We stopped at the bottom of the hill for a rest before climbing the rocks. Suddenly, there directly above us was a huge leopard sitting on a rock looking down at us. We stood motionless for several minutes, and then the animal got up and strolled off into the bush.

"Wow!" said Assigid, imitating the way his tour group would have responded to seeing the leopard.

Mehrab and I didn't say "Wow!" but instead we

talked about the animal and how lucky we had been all the way back to camp. We had seen two leopards. Once we were busy with leopards we hadn't planned to go after any other animals, but on the long walk to the kopjes each day we always saw deer and wild pigs and, on one day, a fox. On another day, some distance from the camp, we thought we spotted a brown bear through the binoculars.

"Woops – we don't want him to come this way, do we, Mehrab?" said Assigid. Then he answered his own question as he must have done hundreds of times before to clients because he thought it was funny: "It's only a bear and he won't bother us. He a good bear. In this area all the time. Rubbish hole over there. That's why he come for your new rubbish. No tourists come, he get hungry. He welcome you. Watch him – he will wave. I will wave and then he will wave."

Extraordinary as it may seem, the bear did wave. It must have all started one day in the past when he was trying to get remains out of a tin and had thrown the tin in the air and stretched his paw upward to catch the tin's contents. Assigid had waved at him, congratulating him. Ever since, the bear associated the action of Assigid waving as a trigger for him to throw a tin up, whether half empty or full, and put his paw up to catch the contents as it fell. We could hardly see the small tin, but we could see his big paw stretched upwards to catch the food – a bear wave.

Assigid said, "When I with big tourist group I introduce bear differently. I tell them if we want to see bear wave we must put some money in my bag, then he will wave. Bear has never let me down."

Mehrab and I laughed, but we didn't put any money in his bag. Instead we all marvelled at the bear's antics and how bears could easily learn.

The early morning of the day we had to leave I woke feeling very disturbed and unhappy and I was pleased to find that Mehrab was already awake. In fact he was just waking me. He was gently pulling at one of my nipples. I was completely relaxed, even though what he was doing surprised me. I was a bit distracted, dreaming and wishing he wasn't always travelling away to distant places.

Suddenly be became aggressive and yelled out, "Damn you, Gracie – I love you."

I was taken by surprise and was a little scared. I knew he meant it.

"I love you," he repeated, and then impatiently he rammed his penis into me and it burst into life.

Later, on his way to the shower, he suddenly felt guilty about how rough he had been and he said he hoped he hadn't hurt me. He hadn't often mentioned to me the passion and hunger he had for me. This had been a very passionate moment, he couldn't help it. He apologised because of the discussion we had at the lake a few days before.

"Honey," I replied, "I enjoy strong deep thrusts, and the only real pain I have ever had in my life was giving birth to my stillborn. We have been waiting for the 'perfect moment', and that was the 'perfect moment'. It was wonderful. You are wonderful."

He got back into the bed and lay down.

I laughed. "So is that it?"

"I just want to lie beside you. I have something to tell you, honey," he said. "When we get back to the hotel, I have to go away again for three months. The good news, though, is that it will be my very last trip."

I didn't say anything to start with, just stared at him and then smiled and said, "If only I could be, baby, where you are going."

We dawdled along on the journey back on the lake, and Mehrab told me a little about where he was going on this last trip. I was comforted by him telling me about his upcoming journey, as he had never talked about his trips to me before. He said that he was going to fly to an island in the Pacific and take a small plane to a town on the far side of the island at the mouth of a big river, the Pikes river, where Sir Arnold Pikes, an ornithologist, had spent most of his life studying the forest birds.

"That's not what I shall be doing," he laughed.

He explained that he wanted to spend time on that river buying artefacts. He knew he would be able to sell them in the hotel and in one of his bazaar shops once the war was over at home. If he was lucky, he said, he would come across some valuable stuff for sale and he could set himself up for life with the proceeds.

"For you, my Gracie, and me."

He had been tipped off that there were some very rare and valuable ancient carvings in a couple of the villages along the river. It sounded exciting, but I didn't like 'he had been tipped off' or 'very rare and valuable ancient carvings'. If he had been buying valuable, rare artefacts in indigenous villages, tucked away in thick rainforest, maybe he really had been disguising himself on what might have been dangerous trips. It all scared me.

"Goodness," I said. "Is that the sort of thing you often do when you leave me behind? Do you really go so far away? I am beginning to understand why you go away for so long."

"No, Gracie, this is an unusual trip. But, yes, I often travel to the other side of the world on my normal job. It doesn't take long these days with jet aeroplanes."

"I'm glad I didn't know that before or I would have been terrified every time you left. What on earth do you do? I hope you haven't bitten off more than you can chew and that you know when it's time to give up. Do you ever travel disguised sometimes – false papers, the lot – and can you honestly say you change your look because of the change in the weather?"

"Babe, I won't do anything stupid. I promise. We have too much to lose."

He left it at that, but he hadn't answered my question.

Four months later I sat in my room at the hotel sending yet another email. I had been emailing Mehrab nearly every day and he had often replied – sometimes with just one word, but with that at least I knew he was alive. Now he had stopped replying to me completely. If I didn't hear from him by the end of the week, I had decided I would go to look for him on the Pikes river.

"Have you married someone and don't want to write any more? Please change your mind. I miss you.

If I don't get your reply to this email by the weekend, I am coming to look for you."

There was no answer from him. I packed up my room, stuffing everything I owned into the two huge cupboards, and locked the cupboard doors. Then came the difficult part of having to tell Hamid I was going away for a few weeks. I didn't want to alarm him or any of the staff by saying I might never return. I played it as everyday as possible, giving Hamid the keys to the cupboards and my room key.

"Don't let anyone else into Room 111," I joked.

In fact, I felt very unsure about everything – very nervous about my plan to fly away, leaving the hotel, my friends, my life, to go canoeing up a river I had never heard of. It was worrying not to know what was in store for me and heartbreaking to leave not only my new home, but Mehrab's home as well – the hotel. I couldn't rest until I had made the trip to try to find out what had happened to him. Besides, it wasn't the most ridiculous thing I had ever done in my life. But it would be the most important thing.

PART TWO

When I disembarked from the national flight in Kawew, I saw a six-seater Aztec loading to go somewhere. It looked as if it would soon be ready to leave. The pilot was standing on the boarding steps.

"Do you want a ride to Magram?" he yelled. "I have a couple of free seats. If you were thinking of canoeing up the Pikes river, Magram is the best starting point. I fly there twice every day. Today I have no passengers, just freight – hence the empty seats."

"That sounds great – canoeing up the Pikes is exactly what I had in mind, so no point in hanging around here, especially if you are offering me a free seat. Definitely no point in hanging around here. Mind you, don't drop me off somewhere sinister and refuse to take me further unless I pay you a huge sum of money. I've heard stories like that about the canoes on the Pikes, arranging a good price in Magram, then getting dumped on a sandbank in the middle of the river at the mercy of crocodiles if you refuse to pay extra once the journey starts."

"No, I wouldn't do that to a cool Sheila like you,"

the pilot laughed. "Well, I wouldn't ask for money – maybe something else?" He laughed again.

I grabbed my bag and as I walked passed him I laughed too, lifted my head and said to him, "Bloody Aussie."

During the fifty-minute flight I sat ruminating about the stories of the famous Pikes river, running about 1,000 kilometres from its source in the mountains to the sea. The mountains were covered with magnificent tropical rainforests.

"Just the sort of nature that is my second best," I remembered telling Mehrab when we were sailing peacefully across Lake Plato a few months ago.

That had been a special trip. I had been convinced that we were going to spend many more such trips and much more special time together. Now everything had changed and Mehrab was gone.

I was going to be searching the endless river bends and lagoons for him. Apparently the eerie lagoons supported a dying population of birds of paradise. I wondered if their call sounded like the wind in the shrouds of the sailing boats, as I had imagined when we were tied up at the jetty the night before we set sail on that magical lake trip.

I had heard that the indigenous people in the area hunted these beautiful birds for their plumage, using the feathers to decorate masks, their hairstyles and their bodies. Mehrab had recently said to me, "I would love to cover you with my body" – I laughed to myself and imagined him there so I could say, "Well, Mehrab, why don't you cover me with these beautiful feathers instead?" I knew he would have laughed with me.

Tribes on the Pikes were of different cultures and spoke over 250 languages. Both Mehrab and I would have a problem handling so many. The way of life of all these people was hard going too, as well as the languages. I had read that some people live in villages where houses are built on long stilts sticking up out of the river to protect them from flooding in torrential rain. What a silent, timeless existence that would be, among all the mosquitoes and crocodiles!

The whole area is home to hundreds of indigenous artists, and it is one of the most profuse art-producing regions in the world. Woodcarvers and potters make masks, shields and drums that are still used in mysterious rituals. Their canoes are made from long hollowed-out tree trunks, with totem animals and birds carved on the canoe prows. Some pieces can still be found that are more than 100 years old. Most of the work for sale nowadays is for tourists, but well made. Only experienced dealers can spot the difference between the modern work and that created long ago for tribal ceremonies. Is that what Mehrab was searching for – original pieces of tribal art?

A crowd of people from a nearby village ran across the dirt runway to greet the passengers as we climbed down the plane steps. I could see the best thing to do would be to ask the pilot not only about accommodation for a couple of nights, but also how to hire someone reliable with a canoe to take me on my journey.

"Well . . . um . . . sorry – what's your name, mate?" I asked the pilot. "I'm Gracie."

"Andrew," the pilot replied, adding, with a snigger, that most people called him randy Andy. He went on to say that if I wanted to ask about accommodation, there were two small hotels to choose from: the River View and the Shak. As the River View was closed for the time being, he suggested I try the Shak. "Over there," he said, and pointed. "It is owned by a guy called Mr Sam. He's a local Pikes tribal bloke. Now, if you look over my shoulder, you'll see his son."

He pointed again, this time at a young man nearby, who waved to him. Andy beckoned and the young man came across and shook hands with us.

"Hello," he said. "My name is Tin Man. People call me Tin Man because I make music on a variety of different-sized empty tins. The tourists love it. I'm Sam's son. Shall we walk over to the Shak? It's just over there on the edge of the village and we can discuss your plans."

This was obviously the routine for all the tourists that landed in Magram.

"Well, that was easy, Andy. Thank you very much for your help," I said.

"My pleasure, Gracie." Then he turned to Tin Man: "Hey, you look after Gracie properly and find her a reliable canoe driver to take her up the river."

"Sure, Andy. Sam and Betay will do their very best."

He and I walked off towards the Shak. Sam saw us coming and called to someone inside to meet us.

"Hello, ma'am. I'm Betay."

She spoke very good English and was obviously of Indian origin, a modern Indian woman.

"Betay, it's a pleasure to meet you. I'm Gracie."

"Come inside and we can talk about your plans."

The Shak was a well-built bamboo structure with an open eating area, a lounge and ten double rooms plus three communal bathrooms and three toilets.

"Let's sit in the lounge – not so many flies," said Betay.

Sam popped his head around the door to say hi. Tin Man had gone back towards the plane. I was relieved that it was just the two of us making the arrangements. I had been feeling very nervous about everything, but I felt confident in Betay's presence. I had no intention of telling Betay what I was really up to. I told her the story of the recent loss not only of my family, but of my baby too. I told her I was taking a holiday to give me a chance to come to terms with the tragedies and all the gloom and sadness that surrounded me. I planned to stay a couple of nights at the Shak if possible and then take a canoe with a reliable driver/guide up the Pikes river, visiting and staying in villages and getting to know the local people. I asked Betay if she could organise that for me.

Betay laughed. "That's easy," she said. "I will take you in that canoe over there – the one with a big outboard motor. We need a good motor to get up the more boring parts of the river quickly. In some places on the river the salvinia weed is thick like a carpet, and again the big motor is the only one to take us through the weed. I will take you. I'd love to do that."

"Really?" I said, rather surprised at her reply.

Was she offering to be the driver and the guide? It was like being introduced to myself. Betay was offering to do what I'd been doing a good part of my life – taking visitors on the trip of their lifetime. But Betay used a canoe. I didn't think that would be as simple as driving a Land Rover.

"Well, I do the trip often with guests. I am the best person for it. I have been away holidaying for quite a long time and need to get back to work, getting my teeth into something before the busy season starts. Sam is taking the opportunity to do some Shak repairs and Tin Man is around to take any short trips that come up. Marcus, my older son, works at the River View as a jack of all trades. We don't see much of him. We all try to keep to ourselves in this small, competitive community."

I was happy to hear about the family and was curious about how Sam and Betay had got together. Her English was excellent – much better than Mehrab's. She seemed efficient and knowledgeable, and from the way she talked about navigating the river I assumed she would be a master canoe driver. With her strong, athletic physique she would be expert at poling the canoe too.

"Where did you meet Sam, Betay? He is from around here, isn't he? But you aren't."

Betay told me that she had met him on a cruise ship when she was holidaying on her own years ago. He was the ship's engineer. She was very relaxed and I felt that there was not much more I could wish for, so I agreed to take up the offer of going with Betay. Two nights at the Shak and then we would go up the Pikes in the big canoe for a couple of weeks looking for Mehrab.

We set off in the early morning a couple of days later. The mist was still hanging over the river and it was cold. I shivered, feeling tense, thinking about the real purpose of the trip. I tried to convince myself that I must make the most of the trip and enjoy it, whether I found Mehrab or not. If my emotions got the better of me I would be numb to any possibilities that presented themselves. I had to be lively and receptive and determined. Nevertheless I felt scared as I clambered into the huge canoe. Betay had already arranged the canoe in a clever way. She had two camp chairs in the middle, facing each other. In between us was a tuck box, as she called it – a large tin trunk that carried all the food and belongings. It was perfect for keeping everything dry, especially when the outboard motor was running at high speed, because the prow of the canoe came up out of the water, spraying water everywhere. Without the tin trunk it would have been impossible to keep things dry. She told me that sometimes she made the river trip alone to buy artefacts from the villages along the way that she could sell to her clients. She asked me if it would be OK if she did some buying as we went along. That was the villagers' custom – to create markets on the riverbank just outside the villages to whet the tourists' appetite as we passed by in the canoe.

"Of course I don't mind, Betay," I assured her. "I don't mind at all. I am so lucky to have you on board – not only the perfect driver and guide, but also a professional artefact guru. It will give me a chance to find out more about the villagers and their way of life."

I felt my heart beating extra-fast as I spoke because what I said was so true: it would give me a chance to find out more about the villagers, and maybe about Mehrab too.

As I had read, the river was bordered by a well-developed rainforest that, I presumed, thrived because of the high rainfall and volcanic soil. I was anxious to spot some birds of paradise that lived in the thick, humid forest. Many of them were endemic in the area. Because of their bright colours, I expected to get a glimpse of them easily.

Betay laughed at my enthusiasm. "Along the river here you will be lucky to see any because plumage hunters have long since cleared this easy-to-get-to area. If you fancy taking a day away from the river, I can employ a village guide to take us on a bird-of-paradise hunt a few miles deeper into the forest. What do you think?"

It sounded very exciting, if not a bit offtrack from what I had planned, so I turned the offer down. Also, I imagined that bugs and mosquitoes would be numerous, just as they were when we stayed in the villages. The village houses were built on short stilts so that the families could make use of the shade under the buildings on the hot humid days. Of course, if the houses were built in the water, they would have long stilts with rickety walkways to other houses as well as to the riverbank. There was no way that villagers could control the mosquitoes. When the house was built on the riverbank a slow fire was made in the sitting area under the house so the smoke permeated throughout the building. It was a suffocating experience, which

I never came to terms with. We had mosquito nets but they didn't cure the mosquito problem. The net did stop the rats. All the food, like dried fish and grain, was stored upstairs in the sleeping area. As soon as it got dark the rats were everywhere. Betay was impervious to it all. I found night time was not a good time to sleep, and I always longed for daybreak when we climbed back into the canoe. With Betay in charge, within a few minutes I would be fast asleep. If it weren't for the crocodiles I would have preferred to sleep in our big canoe.

One evening, when Betay was buying artefacts from the villagers, I set off to scout around. As usual I had a youngster who spoke a bit of English accompanying me on a tour around the huts. He encouraged me to go with him a bit further afield and led me to a small inlet, shallow and full of thick mud. There was an old canoe across the inlet, making a bridge to the other bank.

The boy ran ahead and called back: "C'mon, matey. You cross."

"No problem," I called back, and started across the old canoe. At that moment something like a wasp stung me on the leg. I bent down to swat it. That started the canoe rocking. I lost my balance and fell, splat, like a big frog into the thick mud below. My little friend was beside himself with laughter as I dragged myself across the inlet to catch up with him.

"Matey, last time I come here with man. He did same – splat." The boy couldn't control his laughter.

I asked him more about it: "When was that? Was he

a young, strong, good-looking man? Long hair? Short hair?"

"Yeah, nice man, Dagreasy, strong fella, give me money, now long time. Long hair, big nose."

"Betay with you then?"

I was excited. Maybe it was Mehrab.

"No Betay – another boy like me. Don't know him." He put his head on his hand to think. "Betay gone away. You know Dagreasy?"

"No," I said.

I didn't want to discuss it any further – not with Betay either. The chances it was Mehrab were very small and I felt I shouldn't keep asking questions, but keep my secret to myself. If it was Mehrab, he may have been up to no good. I had to be careful because I had no idea where he was or what exactly he was up to.

The mud was starting to harden on my skin and I suggested we find some clear, safe, crocodile-free inlet so I could wash. Then we went back across the canoe without incident.

The boy said, "You give me money now."

'Little devil,' I thought.

There must have been a wasps' nest in the old canoe. He brought everyone to cross the inlet and everyone disturbed some wasps in doing so. He hoped someone would get stung and fall in the mud so he could help. Generally people would give him a penny because he was such a little rogue. I gave him some coins and giggled with him. He knew that I knew what he was up to. I felt happy and curious. It had been a good walk, and maybe after a few more days on the river I might find I was on Mehrab's trail.

Every day canoe after canoe loaded with artefacts passed us on the river going in the opposite direction on their way to Magram, where, according to Betay, trucks would be waiting to transport the cargo to sell in all the tourist towns. Surely most of these artefacts had been carved recently and were not what Mehrab was looking for. However, something valuable could be hidden under the huge piles of tourist artefacts. I wondered how many illegal artefacts he was planning to buy and if he was driving one of the loaded canoes. The river was so wide it would be difficult to see someone you knew, even if you had planned a rendezvous.

At the end of the first week an old man in one of the villages we were visiting approached us and asked us if we would like to go with him to one of the village huts and look at some ancient ceremonial carvings hidden in there.

Betay was hesitant and said, "How can you take us to see ceremonial carvings? Women are not allowed to see these things."

"Madam, my name is Fez. The carvings are in my private hut. I am in charge of the place. Village women do not visit this hut because they might suffer some affliction if they do. You are women from overseas, so the rule doesn't apply to you."

He was a very well-spoken friendly man and I was keen to see what he was talking about.

"Shall we go in and look, Betay?" I asked. "I should

love to see some ancient traditional carvings that are believed to have magic powers."

I thought to myself, 'That is exactly what Mehrab would be after. Maybe there will be more evidence of him and his whereabouts inside the hut.'

"OK," said Betay.

We followed Fez into the dark mud hut. It was difficult to see anything as there were only a few candles burning. The room was damp and smelly. Fez lit two oil lamps and gave one to Betay and one to me. He took us across to the corner of the room and pointed out a large wooden carving that had a twisted body with a hook on the end – possibly a ceremonial hook from somewhere on the Pikes. The face was horrific – more so because it was partially eaten away by termites. It seemed to be screaming in pain. One of the legs was broken, too. It seemed to foretell a terrifying story of horror, of someone's future.

Whilst Fez talked to Betay, I cast my eye over a skull lying not far away from the twisted body. It had been carved and inlaid with tiny ivory beads and various small shells. It was an exciting work, fascinating and full of energy.

"This looks much more like the sort of artefact Mehrab is looking for – a heavily beaded human skull with shell inlay. Very beautiful ivory beadwork too," I said to myself.

Fez left Betay and rushed over to me.

"No, madam, don't waste your time with that. It is no longer for sale. It has been signed for and we are waiting for it to be collected. Meanwhile it is safe here. The skull will protect the rightful owner from all accidents and danger. You are not going to be the owner, so you cannot have it."

"Oh!"

I tried to sound disappointed. Could the buyer have been Mehrab? If so, why hadn't he taken it with him? I asked Fez why it hadn't been collected.

"Well," he replied, "he wants to buy this twisted hook as well." He pointed to the frightening ceremonial hook. "He plans to pick them both up at the same time in the not-too-distant future."

"What are you dreaming about, Gracie?"

Betay brought me back to life, so to speak, reminding me that it was time to go and get things sorted out ready for an early morning start.

The next day as we pushed further up the river Betay mentioned Fez again: "Gracie, don't you think Fez is a very intelligent, well-spoken man for this neck of the woods?"

"Yeah, and there was something very different about him. I had the feeling he was more of a visitor, like us, and not a permanent Pikes man. Maybe he has a home elsewhere and only visits to do business here, not living here all the time. He may have a resident offsider here."

"Funny you say that, Gracie, because in the village here they call him Mr Absent. I used to think they were saying 'Absinthe', implying that he drank a lot of alcohol. But how would they know about absinthe unless they have a local brew which they have named the same? Then one villager told me that Fez doesn't spend all his time here. He takes and sells artefacts all over the world."

"That sounds fishy," I laughed as we headed for a wide area of thick salvinia.

Betay said, "In these farthest reaches of the Pikes there is salvinia everywhere–"

"Just like the water lilies on Lake Plato," I interrupted, and I gave a short description of the lake and water lilies, being careful not to mention Mehrab.

Betay had other things on her mind, and at that moment she turned off the outboard motor and handed a pole to me.

"One for you and one for me. Your water lilies wouldn't choke the lake like this salvinia chokes all these waterways. We are in for a slow journey now, Gracie, poling most of our way to the final village, where we can relax for a couple of days before we start the journey home."

Betay was strong and well accustomed to poling. I couldn't match her. The salvinia became very dense and we ground to a halt. There was no way through. We were stuck. We spotted a young boy and girl fishing from a little canoe some distance away and we waved and shouted. We hoped the children were bored with fishing and would find it more fun cutting a way through to us to help us out of the weed. They did. They took a couple of machetes from the bottom of their canoe and started to chop a way through the weed. They worked very hard and made a narrow channel that they could pole through in their little canoe, and they reached us in no time at all.

Then Betay started the outboard motor and we slowly made our way through, widening the channel as we went by, flattening more of the salvinia weed with our big canoe. It was all much more fun for them than fishing. They insisted that they would escort us to the village to make sure we had no more problems.

"What are your names?" I asked as we motored along slowly, towing the little canoe.

The boy, bold and cheeky, answered, pointing to his sister: "This one Mary. She always wash visitors' feet before they enter our house, like some lady wash Jesus' feet. So we call her Mary, like Jesus' lady."

His English was good and it was obvious they had a missionary school in the village. Betay confirmed that.

"It is the biggest village on the pikes and during the tourist season the river up here is crawling with motor boats and canoes with visitors all spending a night or two in the traditional-style village hotels."

"So what is your name?" I asked the boy.

"My name is Dagreasy."

I was startled.

"Why Dagreasy?" I asked, remembering that I had heard that name mentioned before by the boy who had led me across the canoe where the wasps lived, near a previous village.

"I like him – my fave tourist always. I be him one day – big, strong, long oil hair, sharp nose. Clever Dagreasy use his sharp nose very well and wink well." He winked at me.

'That was a Mehrab wink,' I thought.

What a strange story! The name Dagreasy – was that what he called himself here on the river? Or was it meant to be Dagracy, but the kids called him Dagreasy because of his long oily hair. Whatever, it seemed that

Mehrab had been all this way. I asked Betay if she had ever heard of a bloke called Dagreasy whom all the children seemed to know.

"Never – it's just something kids do, hear something and copy it, and pass it on, village to village. Besides, as I said, this area will be crawling with tourists in a couple of weeks, the same as each year. So if there is such a person I should be unlikely to know him. It's a kids' game they play with tourists. I am not involved in that kind of thing because I am a local here."

Betay and I had become good friends. I found her very down to earth and very knowledgeable about the river and the villagers. We enjoyed the days together, especially when Betay went shopping on the riverbank and shared her knowledge about the artefacts with me. It was always on the tip of my tongue to tell her about Mehrab and how he was meant to have been searching the Pikes villages for some ancient woodcarvings or any cultural objects. But I didn't, because I really had no idea about what he was doing or even where he was. He had sounded very honest about his proposed plans and I had never doubted him. That is why I had travelled to the Pikes to try to find him. But maybe he wasn't trustworthy. I wouldn't have made the journey if there wasn't some sort of chance of finding out something about him. Maybe the Dagreasy stories by the village boys were a game, but I believed that Mehrab had been travelling in the area just as he had said he would.

I wondered if Mehrab had bought the ornamental skull, but I couldn't make head or tail of the reason why he had decided to go back later to collect it and not take it with him. That made me think it wasn't him at all. It occurred to me that Fez was probably a psychopath. He sold a ceremonial artefact, like the engraved skull, took the money and then disposed of the buyer. Easy to do with the big river right there full of hungry crocodiles. He then kept the artefact to sell over and over again, thereby making himself a fortune. I didn't want to think about that possibility; nor did I want to suggest any of my paranoid ideas to my friend Betay.

  I hadn't done a huge search for Mehrab, but I had made some discoveries on the journey. I had found two boys in separate villages who could easily have met him, judging by their descriptions of him and the name they called him. They called him Dagreasy, perhaps because of his greasy hair. His surname was actually Dagracy, so either the kids couldn't pronounce that properly or they called him Dagreasy on purpose, because of his hair. I had got a feel of the place and believed I knew pretty well that if he had been here some weeks ago, anything could have happened to him since.

  I tried to clear my mind, relax and enjoy the journey back down the river. I remembered Mehrab – everything about him from the time we met at the airport. We had shared great happiness and had so many more plans for times to come. I had always spent time imagining how all those future plans would pan out, and I felt I must go on imagining those things, as well as the fact that we would meet again one day. I didn't know how I could manage life if I gave up being positive. Sometimes as I lay under my mosquito-ridden net at night, when Betay was asleep, I sobbed endlessly and longed to be able to have him hold me tight so I could feel the warmth of his body and know that my nightmare was over.

We got back to Magram to find that Betay had received a tour booking for a group of ten Irish people to travel on the river for five days. That meant a large amount of preparation. For a start, finding good canoes and getting Tin Man and his friends to make themselves available for the trip. Sam had already got the accommodation ready. Betay asked me if I would mind staying at the River View. Although it wasn't yet open for tourists, Rathore, the owner, had invited me to stay there. I realised how spoilt I had been to share the canoe with just Betay, and to have had the whole Shak to myself. I was happy to stay at the River View for a few days before I made my way home though. It was a beautiful spot on the river. I hugged Betay and we laughed because all of a sudden our journey was over. It had been wonderful to have her there every day, a real silent support, although she didn't realise it.

"Here today and gone tomorrow," said Betay. "I can't keep up with you gadabouts."

'I can't either,' I thought. 'Mehrab, you must slow down or I'll never catch up with you.'

I thought the River View would be a good spot to end the journey. I felt despondent – so many ups and downs to overcome and no real discoveries, nothing to lead me on to a further search. At the River View I could spend time on the open verandah collecting my thoughts and watching birds and crocodiles splashing in the water. Big crocodiles frequently slunk along the river, preventing villagers from fishing off the riverbank.

Rathore, the hotel owner, tall, greying and attentive, was the perfect host. He had many stories to tell about the river in times gone by, though none of them were very happy stories, being mostly about drownings, people getting eaten by crocodiles and boat accidents. Rathore had a particular way of telling a story so that it didn't seem like a terrible disaster, but just something that happens if you live near a big river. He often managed to find an amusing side to some of the events that had happened long ago when they had faded in his memory somewhat and were just another incident in life.

A young lad called Marcus, probably sixteen years old, was always around checking if I was comfortable, in need of food or something to drink, and he never failed to ask if I was happy. He reminded me of the staff at the Sheer Magic Hotel and that comforted me. I wondered how they were and if everything was going OK for them. Although down in the dumps, the thought of being back at the hotel with them soon excited me. I would be able to talk to them about the journey openly, not always guarding my secret. And I would tell them about Marcus, my new friend – or, as Mehrab would say, my new partner in crime.

Marcus told me he liked to keep an eye on one particular huge crocodile that spent most of its time lying on the bank directly below the middle of the verandah.

One morning when he came to check it, I said very quietly to myself, "Wow, what if a hotel guest fell over the verandah?"

Marcus thought I was talking to him, and he walked close to me as he had not heard what I had said.

"What did you say, madam?"

I was about to repeat the question, but gasped and pointed – not at the crocodile, but at the boy's neck. It was extraordinary. I wondered if I was dreaming. I took a step even closer to Marcus. I was shocked to see my beaded necklace around his neck. It was definitely the same necklace. I had given it to Hamid, who gave it to Mehrab, and now Marcus was wearing it. Fodro, who looked after the boat for us at Lake Plato, had asked Mehrab for it and Mehrab had refused. So where did Marcus get it from? Had Mehrab traded it for a canoe ride or something?

"Where did you get that beautiful necklace from, Marcus?"

"Wait, madam."

And he walked into the building and came back with Rathore.

"It is pretty, isn't it, Gracie? But he won't sell it to you." Rathore laughed sheepishly.

"But, Rathore, where did he get it?"

"It was given to him by his best friend. They share it. Marcus wears it one day and his friend wears it the next day."

I could barely speak.

"His best friend? Who is that?"

Rathore sat down.

"In June, I gave Marcus the job to take a tourist

on a four-week journey up the Pikes river to look for artwork. He was one of those people who want to comb the area and make himself a fortune selling artefacts, like so many other people."

Marcus interrupted: "Especially nasty Fez."

Rathore ignored Marcus and continued: "At the same time the tourist was a top bloke – friendly, kind, honest. Marcus went everywhere with him. They became inseparable. By the way, Marcus is Betay's son. She has been away a lot this off-season, so Marcus was the perfect choice to make an extended trip with Dagracy while Tin Man looked after the short trips up the river. Anyway, let me get back to my story. Dagracy – or Dagreasy, as the river people started calling him – was everyone's hero, a great character, because he was so enthusiastic about life, helping the villagers and playing with the kids."

"Where is he now, Rathore?" I asked. "You keep using the past tense – what does that mean?"

"Marcus and I call him Dag – Dagracy is too long."

I gasped as I remembered Mehrab's voice: "Can I call you Gracie? Ida Grace is such a mouthful?"

"Much too long, so we call him Dag. He and Marcus came back here some time ago to pick up provisions so that they could set off on a final short trip to collect a couple of special things they had bought. One of them is a large object, so they needed a good space in the canoe to carry it safely. Dag dropped Marcus off here to go and shop in the village. Dag took off downriver to buy diesel. I saw him in the distance – he looked very smart with a short haircut. Quite unrecognisable. I thought he was taking on some disguise, as if he was getting into big business, buying some special items. I asked Marcus at the time, but he said, 'Nah, he just gets too hot with all that long hair.' Anyhow, he made his way around the bend in the river. The next thing I heard was an almighty crash. Marcus heard it too and came rushing to get me in the truck. When we reached the fuel-pump area the first thing we saw was Dag floating on the water – thank God he always wore a life jacket. We got to him before the crocodiles did. He was unconscious. We got him out of the water by floating a rubber mattress under him and then took him by truck to the hotel.

"According to the folk that were around there at the fuel pump, when Dag motored in towards the pump there was a big ocean-going yacht in front of him fuelling up. They said it was a visitor's boat and a young guy was in the skipper's seat. Maybe it was being driven by this youngster to refuel it whilst the actual skipper went for lunch with the clients. He apparently was not competent, maybe on drugs. He made a terrible mistake. When Dag had pulled in behind the yacht he made sure a good part of the canoe was floating slightly under the jetty to give the yacht more room to get out. It was not a long wait. Then the youngster started his engine. Instead of manoeuvring his craft slowly and carefully backwards, he put on the power and at a good speed knocked the end of the canoe, crushing it with an enormous thrust under the jetty, smashing it to a pulp. The canoe was unrecognisable and of course Dag was nowhere to be seen. The young skipper climbed out of the yacht and took off down the riverbank with a crowd of people chasing him. He jumped into the river. No one has seen him since. The question remains: was this an accident or was it done purposely by someone who didn't want Dag around any longer?"

"So is Dag dead?" I hardly dared to ask.

"No," said Rathore. "He was unconscious and still is, although he is showing signs of improvement. Once we reached the hotel we did what we could, having contacted the Emergency Flight people. We have a medical box here at the hotel, so we carefully got him cleaned up a bit and cut some of the wet clothes off him. Bandaged him in places. He seemed to have so many wounds. He had severe deep wounds across his head and face, maybe a broken neck, cracked skull, a partly severed leg. We didn't know exactly what but we got him on to a firm, warm bed. The next day the medics arrived. They didn't want to move him with all those injuries, but they stayed here for a couple of days fixing him up and making him as comfortable as possible. They taught Marcus and me a routine caring procedure. I think they thought he would die quite soon."

I wanted to know all the details, but I couldn't think of anything to say. I didn't even know if it was Mehrab.

I was shocked and speechless, but suddenly blurted out, "Well, did he die? I may know who he is. I came a long way to look for him. When I saw the beads on Marcus I knew he must be here somewhere. I gave that necklace to him. He's my friend and his name is Mehrab."

"Isn't his name Dagracy?" asked Rathore.

I explained that it wasn't, but that his full name was

Mehrab Dagracy-Roberts and that most people called him Mehrab. I asked again if he had died.

"No, he didn't die. But he is only semi-conscious. He rarely opens his eyes and he is basically living in his own world. He is also paralysed on one side and has a partially severed leg. Not as many injuries as we originally thought. You must go to see him, Gracie. Marcus will come with you."

Rathore showed no emotion. 'Just another river accident for him,' I thought.

I started to cry. Everything was too much for me. Marcus came across the room and put his arm around my shoulders.

"Come with me, Gracie. He talked to me about you every day when we were travelling. I feel I already know you."

The door was open so I crept in and there he was, lying on his back, not moving, but his eyes were wide open.

Did he wink? I wondered. If he had winked I would know he had an idea who I was and who he was, even though he looked so helpless. I felt an enormous sense of relief. It was Mehrab and he was alive. I had to do whatever I could to help him recover. I sat on the chair beside his bed and held his limp hand, not knowing if he could hear or see me.

Rathore asked me to extend my stay, and the three of us became a strong team doing whatever we could for him each day. I would sit by him when I was drawing or reading. I was in love with him and never wanted to think about how he used to be. This was my darling Mehrab. At night I put my camp bed beside him and held his hand and quietly sang his favourite songs to him. Whether he knew about any of these things I didn't know, but I knew I wouldn't leave until it was all resolved.

One afternoon when we were resting Marcus called me and told me there was someone at the door asking for Dagracy. He wanted to give him something. I was uncertain about this. Marcus seemed to know the man and was talking to him at length. He assured me that he did know him. The man told him he knew Gracie as well. When I went out to greet him I recognised him immediately. He was from the old mud ceremonial hut on the Pikes – Fez. The man that Betay and I had been suspicious of.

"Hello, madam. Do you remember me? I heard of this terrible accident and I realised that my friend Dagracy wouldn't be back to pick up his purchases – the wonderful ancient decorated skull and the hook. I have travelled here to give the skull to him and the hook will follow later."

I was astounded by his honesty. From under a robe he was wearing he disclosed the decorated skull from the upper Pikes that presumably Mehrab and Marcus had been on the way back to collect when the accident happened.

He took the skull from its hiding place and gave it to me, saying, "Now Dagracy can die in peace."

He left the house and walked away chanting.

Marcus said he was totally surprised by all of it. Firstly, why didn't Fez use Mehrab's real name, Mehrab, not Dagracy? Fez knew his full name. Mehrab had told Marcus that he and Fez had known each other a long time when he saw him on the Pikes trip and that they had scores to settle. Secondly, how did Fez know Gracie? Thirdly, how did he know that there had been an accident? It was not the right time to go through all this, but he himself, like many people on the river, hated Fez. Nobody trusted him. He was said to deal in precious ceremonial artefacts by the thousands all around the world. Also, he was said to run guns and an organisation that sent mercenaries to governments and businesses anywhere they were needed. Unfortunately for those he employed, he rarely paid for anything. If he did pay, it was never cash but something he had stolen from somewhere else, like an artefact from one country or another. When Mehrab had said he and Fez had a score to settle, Marcus presumed that Mehrab hadn't been paid anything for a large amount of mercenary work. Mehrab had told Marcus he worked as a mercenary, but he didn't mention Fez. He did make Marcus promise that if he ever met Gracie he would not tell her about the mercenary work. But presumably that's why Mehrab was on the river collecting what was due in the form of the ornate skull and twisted hook. Marcus did not trust Fez at all and felt sure that even though he had given the skull to Mehrab he would be sure to try to get it back. The twisted hook was yet to be delivered and as far as Marcus was concerned, Mehrab was better off without it. It was a bad omen with its eaten-away face and broken leg. It hadn't taken Marcus long to recognise that Mehrab had similar injuries, as foretold by the evil hook with the twisted body and horrific screaming expression.

On the bright side, the event of having a visit from Fez and the delivery of the ornate skull had an unexpected effect on Mehrab. He seemed to start making a slow recovery. From then on he began to improve physically and mentally. His memory and speech were noticeably developing. Was everything starting to fall into place for him?

Every day I spent hours chatting to him, reminding him of everything we had done together. He always listened carefully and often smiled and said yes or no or other simple words and sometimes a short phrase. Often he seemed to be trying to tell me something. And then longer sentences showed his memory was improving. It made me feel very happy, although I knew these busy days completely exhausted him because he was silent for the next couple of days. I was impressed by how he began to pull himself up to a sitting position on his own. Next, I found him one day sitting on the side of the bed and I noticed his growing ability to do little things for himself. His speech was clearly showing that his memory was alive, and he would gabble away a bit like a crazy man.

"No disguise, no, no, no. You safe Ida. We side by side."

I always nodded or shook my head – whichever seemed appropriate – and kissed him and squeezed his hand.

Another day when I woke him in the morning he said, "I know you Ida. You are the gracious, sexy lady from the lake." Then another day he said something very curious: "Gracie, that bear man, Assigid, my friend. We mercenaries working together everywhere. Bear man, bear totem, we use gun, not spear. We work everywhere – South America, Papua, Guinea-Bissau."

"What are you saying Mehrab? Are you dreaming? Is this true, that you and Assigid were mercenaries?"

I realised that this could easily be true. That was why he kept going away and it was always a secret, but I couldn't work out the stuff about the bear man, though he was obviously remembering Assigid and the bear raiding the rubbish in the pit. Obviously his gabbling could be very confused as his brain was trying to get back to normal. But who was the person accompanying him on these trips? Not Assigid – he was the bear man. It must have been Fez. The villagers said he sold guns. Would he be smuggling guns to a neighbouring country's uprising and at the same time be spying for that country's government? That way he would be making money from both sides of a fight for independence. All this as well as illegally dealing with ancient ceremonial artefacts! What part did Mehrab play in it?

"None at all," Gracie said to herself. "He may have worked as a mercenary, but illegal dealing in ancient treasures or spying was not what he would do."

She knew that.

In time Mehrab was moved to a hospital in Kawew, where he worked at a strict rehabilitation programme. I enjoyed working with him and admired the way he persevered. We were in this together, supporting each other and both benefitting from it because we knew that the sooner he had reached a certain level of fitness the sooner he would only have to pay daily visits to the hospital. After a short spell there he had greatly improved. He really benefitted from the care of a team of specialist doctors.

He was discharged and came to live at the small flat I had rented. He continued to visit the hospital daily, but came back to the flat at night. Evenings together in the flat were magic, unforgettable as we gradually built up our friendship again.

"It is a miracle, Mehrab, how you have recovered. You'll soon be ready to cover my body with yours like you wanted to do in the national park. I might let you do that this time," I teased.

I was careful not to mention the injury to the bottom half of his left leg, because I knew he was still very conscious of that. There were many other things he didn't like about his head and body, where extensive repairs were still healing and had slightly changed his look. Of course I didn't see the difference, but Mehrab had always been very vain and he apologised for not being as handsome as he used to be. We laughed.

One evening Mehrab told me briefly about his work away from home when he was working for Fez off and on for many years. He mentioned the fact that he had not been paid and that was why he was making his last journey away to meet Fez and pick up an alternative in lieu of a considerable amount of money owed him by Fez. In fact, Fez had been friendly. He had brought the artefact to his bedside. Mehrab didn't care about the twisted hook – just juju, he had thought to himself at the time – and he was only going back to pick it up on the day he had the accident because Fez had told him he could only have the skull if he took the hook as well and they wouldn't fit in his loaded canoe on the first journey.

Then he told me that now he didn't want to go anywhere without me. We would sell the ornate skull to a reputable art museum in the USA and we would travel together far and wide to look for a place to buy; or, if the situation had improved we might buy the Sheer Magic Hotel, our hotel, where we met, and settle down.

"By the way, babe, where is the skull?" Mehrab asked.

"I have already sold it," I laughed.

He got up and caught me and pinned me down, holding me tight and covering my face with little kisses.

"That's OK. We'll just have to live a poor man's life – we're used to that. It doesn't matter as long as we are together. Now, tell me, where is the skull?" He winked. "If you tell me the truth I'll—"

"In my big art-materials case under the bed over there."

I pointed, giggling because I didn't think he would be able to get under the bed. But he did scramble under the bed and checked it out.

"Honey, I am better now, so watch your step." He grinned as he came to sit beside me on the sofa, and gently pushed me down saying, "Now you've told me the truth I'll remind you of our last morning in the Village National Park."

"Wow, but first you tell me where is the bead necklace?"

He replied that he had left it with Marcus. He wanted him to have it.

Finally he was finished with hospital visits and we were free to go home. One evening we managed to get through to Hamid on the phone, and Mehrab told him we were on our way back to the hotel soon so he must get the house in order. He replied that life had much improved in the last couple of months and the hotel was very busy. That was very good news. We were excited about the future and all that lay in store for us. The following week we were up early loading the taxi. We were on our way, happy and excited about being together for the rest of our lives. In the taxi we were discussing our favourite names for children. It didn't take long to drive to the airport. When the taxi stopped I made sure I had a good hold of my art-materials case.

On the short walk to the terminal someone suddenly called Mehrab's name. He turned round to see a man wrapped in a blanket carrying a bundle. The man stretched out to give it to Mehrab; but Mehrab didn't get hold of it because the cloth it was wrapped in fell off in the wind and the object fell to the ground. I screamed as I suddenly saw the horrific hook again, the termite-damaged head and screaming face, and the severed left leg. Mehrab turned sideways to comfort me, but fell backwards into my arms, dead. The man had stabbed Mehrab in the chest.

I heard someone chanting like Fez.